OXFORD
UNIVERSITY PRESS

Great Clarendon Street, Oxford, OX2 6DP

Oxford University Press is a department of the University of Oxford.
It furthers the University's objective of excellence in research, scholarship,
and education by publishing worldwide in

Oxford New York

Auckland Bangkok Buenos Aires Cape Town Chennai
Dar es Salaam Delhi Hong Kong Istanbul Karachi Kolkata
Kuala Lumpur Madrid Melbourne Mexico City Mumbai Nairobi
São Paulo Shanghai Taipei Tokyo Toronto

Oxford is a registered trade mark of Oxford University Press
in the UK and in certain other countries

British Library Cataloguing in Publication Data available

ISBN 0-19-279090 0 (hardback)
ISBN 0-19-272542 4 (paperback)

1 3 5 7 9 10 8 6 4 2

Printed in Malaysia

The Tortoise
and the Hare

Ian Beck

OXFORD
UNIVERSITY PRESS

Once upon a time, and as long ago as anyone can remember, there lived a tortoise. His was a slow, steady, and pleasant life. Every winter, while the world was cold and harsh, he would fill up on sweet lettuce and carrots, and then fall fast asleep in his cosy home.

Just near the tortoise lived an excitable and bouncy hare. He rushed everywhere at great speed, especially in the spring, when he seemed to be full of extra energy.

So it was one bright morning, when the hare rushed past his neighbour the tortoise on the road. The tortoise had been ambling along, minding his own business. He had only just woken up from his long winter sleep, and was just getting used to the world again, when he was nearly knocked over by the dashing hare.

'Hey, watch where you're going,' said the tortoise. 'We can't all rush about like you.'

'My word,' said the hare, 'but you are a slow-coach.'

Now the tortoise was cross at having been nearly knocked over, and he answered quite snappily, 'Not as slow as you seem to think. Why, I could beat you in a race any day.'

'Oh, really,' said the hare with a laugh. 'I wouldn't bet on it if I were you.'

Just then a fox strolled past, and the hare said to him, 'This tortoise says he can beat me in a race!' At this the hare and the fox laughed and laughed which made the tortoise even crosser.

He said, 'I bet you my snug winter den that I can beat you over any distance.'

'And I'll bet *you* a lifetime supply of sweet lettuce and carrots that you can't,' said the hare.

Then the fox had an idea. 'Why don't you run a race?' he said. 'I shall judge the winner.'

'Agreed,' said the tortoise and the hare together, and the hare added, 'Easiest bet I've ever won,' and laughed again.

The tortoise said nothing. He just smiled and shook his head.

So it was that the fox set up a course across the countryside with a start and finish line, and the next morning the tortoise and the hare lined up ready to race.

The fox raised his flag, and said, 'Ready!' The hare raised himself up on his strong back legs, but the tortoise just stood and waited.

Then the fox said, 'Steady!' The hare puffed out his cheeks, but the tortoise just stood and waited.

At last the fox said, 'Go!' and the hare sprinted away as fast as he could.

The tortoise just ambled forward in his slow and steady way.

The hare ran fast for a while. Then he slowed a little and looked down the road. There was no sign of the tortoise. He had been left far behind. The hare laughed to himself and stopped altogether. It was a warm morning, and running so fast was tiring work.

The hare spotted a nice patch of shade under a tree, and he went and sat there to wait for the tortoise.

'It'll be a long wait,' he said to himself, and yawned and stretched. 'I'll just have a little nap.'

He settled under the tree and soon fell fast asleep.

The tortoise walked along, sure and steady. It was very warm, and he was hot, so he stopped for a nibble of cooling dandelion leaves.

The sun rose higher and hotter, but the tortoise ambled on, slow but sure. Slowly he overtook a snail.

'Morning, Mr Snail,' said the tortoise.

'Morning, Mr Tortoise,' said the snail. 'If you look over there you can see the hare asleep under that tree.'

'Why, so he is,' said the tortoise, and he smiled and shook his head and carried on, and on, down the dusty road.

The hare woke from his
refreshing nap. He felt fine, if a
little stiff. He stretched
and ran up and down for
a bit to ease himself in
for the run.
Then he jumped up and
down, to warm himself up.
'I'll just
see how
far ahead
of the tortoise I am,'
he thought, and
climbed the tree to
look back down the road.
There was no sign of
the tortoise but he
could just see a snail,
far away.

He turned round, and in the distance far off he could see the finish line with its bright banner, and a crowd of animals waiting.

He was about to jump down and do some push-ups before setting off again, when he saw something on the road that almost made him fall out of the tree in shock.

It was the tortoise plodding along towards the finish line!

Amazed, the hare set off again
as fast as
he could.
He crested
the hill,
and there,
way ahead of
him, was
the tortoise, making
steady progress, now only a
few feet away from the finish line. The hare
made one last great effort and charged down
the final straight.

He crossed the line and fell, out of breath,
to the ground.

He was too late.

The tortoise had crossed the line long
before the hare, and was being congratulated
by the fox.

'That's a lifetime of
sweet lettuce and carrots
you owe me,' said the tortoise to the hare,
with a big smile.

The tortoise lived for a very, very, very,
long time (as tortoises do), and for all of
that time the hare had to make sure he had
lots and lots of sweet lettuce and carrots.